EDWARDO

The Horriblest Boy in the Whole Wide World

John Burningham

Red Fox

For Tiny Tom

EDWARDO, THE HORRIBLEST BOY IN THE WHOLE WIDE WORLD
A RED FOX BOOK 978 0 099 48013 6

First published in Great Britain by Jonathan Cape,
an imprint of Random House Children's Books

Jonathan Cape edition published 2006
Red Fox edition published 2007

1 3 5 7 9 10 8 6 4 2

Red Fox Books are published by Random House Children's Books,
61–63 Uxbridge Road, London W5 5SA,
a division of The Random House Group Ltd,
in Australia by Random House Australia (Pty) Ltd,
20 Alfred Street, Milsons Point, Sydney, NSW 2061, Australia,
in New Zealand by Random House New Zealand Ltd,
18 Poland Road, Glenfield, Auckland 10, New Zealand,
in South Africa by Random House (Pty) Ltd,
Isle of Houghton, Corner Boundary Road & Carse O'Gowrie,
Houghton 2198, South Africa,
and in India by Random House India Pvt Ltd,
301 World Trade Tower, Hotel Intercontinental Grand Complex,
Barakhamba Lane, New Delhi 110001, India

THE RANDOM HOUSE GROUP Limited Reg. No. 954009
www.**kids**at**randomhouse**.co.uk

A CIP catalogue record for this book is available from the British Library.

Printed in Singapore

Edwardo was an ordinary boy.

He would get up in the morning,
get dressed, have his breakfast,
go to school, play games,
eat his supper and go to bed.

Sometimes Edwardo would kick things.

'You are a rough boy, Edwardo, you are always kicking things. You are the roughest boy in the whole wide world.' Edwardo became rougher and rougher.

Like most children, Edwardo made a lot of noise.

'You are a very noisy boy, Edwardo. You are the noisiest boy in the whole wide world.'
Edwardo became noisier and noisier.

From time to time Edwardo was nasty to little children.

'You are a nasty bully, Edwardo. You are the nastiest boy in the whole wide world.'
Edwardo became nastier and nastier.

Occasionally Edwardo was not very nice to animals and would chase the cat.

'You are a cruel boy, Edwardo, chasing the cat.
You are the cruellest boy in the whole wide world.'
Edwardo became more and more cruel.

Edwardo was not always good at keeping his room tidy.

'Your room gets messier and messier every day, Edwardo. You are the messiest boy in the whole wide world.'
Edwardo's room became messier and messier.

Often Edwardo would forget to wash his face and brush his teeth in the mornings.

'You are a dirty boy, Edwardo. You are the dirtiest boy in the whole wide world.'

Edwardo became dirtier and dirtier.

And as the days turned into weeks and the weeks into months, Edwardo became even clumsier, crueller, noisier, messier, dirtier, nastier, ruder and rougher until one day they said . . .

'Edwardo, you really are

THE HORRIBLEST BOY

IN THE WHOLE WIDE WORLD.'

Then one day, when Edwardo kicked a pot of flowers,
it flew through the air and landed on some earth.

'I see you are starting a little garden, Edwardo.
It looks lovely. You should get some more plants.'

Edwardo was good at growing things and he was
asked to help people with their gardens.

Cruel Edwardo was waiting for the dog with a bucket of water. He threw it over the dog as it came by.

'Thank you so much, Edwardo, for washing my muddy dog for me. You are so good with animals.'

And so Edwardo was asked to clean and look after
everybody's pets.

Edwardo's room was getting so untidy that he could not find anything, so he threw everything out of the window.

All Edwardo's things landed in a truck that was collecting for poor people.

'Thank you, Edwardo, for giving all of your things away.'

'Look at Edwardo's room. Why can't you all be as neat and tidy as he is?'

Edwardo was becoming dirtier and dirtier until one day he became so dirty that flies started to chase him down the road. He jumped into the river to get away from them.

A lady pulled Edwardo out of the river and took him back to her house. She gave him a hot bath, washed and ironed all his clothes and sent him back to school.

'Look, children. Look at Edwardo. He is the cleanest and smartest boy in the whole school.'

One day, at school, nasty Edwardo pushed little Alec very hard.

At that moment, one of the lights in the room crashed down onto the spot where Alec had been standing.

'You have just saved our little Alec. What a quick-thinking boy you are. You should look after the little ones.'

And from then on Edwardo looked after the little children.

One day Edwardo was making more noise than he had ever made before, which frightened some lions who had escaped.

They were so frightened by noisy Edwardo that they went back to their cage.

'You're very good with lions, Edwardo. Perhaps you could come and help me.'

Now from time to time Edwardo is a little untidy,
cruel, dirty, messy, clumsy, noisy, nasty and rude.
But really Edwardo is . . .